PRO SPORTS SUPERSTARS

Superstars of the NHL

by Todd Kortemeier

AMICUS HIGH INTEREST • AMICUS INK

Amicus High Interest and Amicus Ink
are imprints of Amicus
P.O. Box 1329, Mankato, MN 56002
www.amicuspublishing.us

Library of Congress Cataloging-in-Publication Data
Names: Kortemeier, Todd, 1986-
Title: Superstars of the NHL / by Todd Kortemeier.
Other titles: Superstars of the National Hockey League
Description: Mankato, MN : Amicus High Interest, [2016] | Series: Pro sports superstars |
Includes index.
Identifiers: LCCN 2015033468 (print) | LCCN 2015047896 (ebook) |
ISBN 9781607539384 (hardcover)
ISBN 9781681510286 (pdf ebook)
ISBN 9781681521039 (paperback)
Subjects: LCSH: Hockey players--Biography--Juvenile literature. | Hockey--History--Juvenile literature. | National Hockey League--History--Juvenile literature.
Classification: LCC GV848.5.A1 K68 2016 (print) | LCC GV848.5.A1 (ebook) |
DDC 796.9620922--dc23
LC record available at http://lccn.loc.gov/2015033468

Photo Credits: Robin Alam/Icon Sportswire/AP Images, cover, 4–5; Mike Wulf/Cal Sport Media/AP Images, 2, 14; Charles Hoff/NY Daily News/Getty Images, 6; Manny Millan/Sports Illustrated/Getty Images, 8; Mark Humphrey/AP Images, 10–11; Alex Brandon/AP Images, 12–13, 22; Nam Y. Huh/AP Images, 16; Danny Moloshok/AP Images, 19; Mark J. Terrill/AP Images, 21

Produced for Amicus by The Peterson Publishing Company
and Red Line Editorial.

Editor Arnold Ringstad
Designer Becky Daum

Printed in the United States of America

HC 10 9 8 7 6 5 4 3 2 1
PB 10 9 8 7 6 5 4 3 2

TABLE OF CONTENTS

THE FASTEST GAME ON ICE

Great goals. Big hits. Quick skating. Amazing **saves**. NHL hockey is exciting. The sport is fast-paced. There are many stars. Here are some of the best.

BISHOP
30
2
Reebok
Reebok

GORDIE HOWE

Gordie Howe was known as "Mr. Hockey." He was an early star. His first year was 1946. Howe was a great skater. He was strong. Howe played his last game in 1980. He scored 801 goals. Only one player has more.

WAYNE GRETZKY

Wayne Gretzky was called "The Great One." Some say he's the best hockey player ever. He scored 894 goals. He also made perfect passes. That helped others score. Gretzky was named **MVP** nine times. The last time was in 1989.

Gretzky played in the All-Star Game every season.

SIDNEY CROSBY

Sidney Crosby was called "The Next One." People knew he would be great. He proved it right away. His first year was 2005. He won the MVP award the next year. His team, the Pittsburgh Penguins, won the **Stanley Cup** in 2009.

Crosby was the youngest team captain to win the Cup.

OVECHKIN
8
Reebok
BAUER

ALEXANDER OVECHKIN

Alexander Ovechkin is from Russia. He played hockey there as a boy. He came to the NHL in 2005. He scored 52 goals that year. He won **Rookie** of the Year. Ovechkin was MVP in 2008. He is a great scorer. He led the league in goals five times.

STEVEN STAMKOS

Steven Stamkos scores goals. He also is a great skater. He plays good **defense**. He led the NHL in goals in 2010. He had 51. It was only his second year. He led the league again in 2012. He scored his 250th goal in 2014.

Stamkos is one of the youngest players to score 250 goals.

BAUER
19

JONATHAN TOEWS

Jonathan Toews is captain of the Chicago Blackhawks. He is their leader. He makes his team better. And he can score. He is great in big moments. He helped Chicago win three Stanley Cups. He was MVP of the **playoffs** in 2010.

Toews won two Olympic gold medals. He played for Canada.

COREY PERRY

Corey Perry was MVP in 2011. He scored 50 goals that year. He helps the Anaheim Ducks win. Perry is a big player. He skates well. He has played in three All-Star Games. He has nearly 300 goals.

Hospital
DUCKS

HENRIK LUNDQVIST

Henrik Lundqvist is a great goalie. He plays for the New York Rangers. Lundqvist is very quick. In 2012, he gave up fewer than two goals per game. He stopped 93 percent of the shots he faced.

The NHL has had many great superstars. Who will be next?

RANGERS
BAUER

NHL FAST FACTS

First Games: December 19, 1917

Number of Teams: 30—23 in the United States and 7 in Canada

Oldest Teams: Toronto Maple Leafs and Montreal Canadiens, established in 1917

Number of Games: Each team plays 82 per season

Headquarters: New York City, NY

Trophy: The Stanley Cup, created in 1893

Most Titles: Montreal Canadiens, 23

WORDS TO KNOW

All-Star Game – a game played halfway through the season with special teams made of top stars from across the league

captain – the player chosen as the team's leader and the only player allowed to speak with game officials

defense – keeping the other team from scoring

MVP – Most Valuable Player, an award given to the player who contributed the most to his team

playoffs – a tournament after the regular season to determine the Stanley Cup Champion

rookie – a player in his first season

save – when a goalie stops a shot

Stanley Cup – the trophy won by each year's NHL champions

LEARN MORE

Books

Jordan, Christopher. *We Are the Goal Scorers: The Top Point Leaders of the NHL*. Plattsburgh, NY: Fenn/Tundra, 2013.

Jordan, Christopher. *We Are the Goalies: The Top Netminders of the NHL*. Plattsburgh, NY: Fenn/Tundra, 2013.

Websites

Hockey-Reference.com
http://www.hockey-reference.com
Find statistics about every team and player.

NHL.com
http://www.nhl.com
Learn the latest news from around the league.

INDEX